P9-CKW-217

We Will Live in This Forest Again

NEAL PORTER BOOKS
HOLIDAY HOUSE / NEW YORK

We have always lived
in this forest.

Its trees and shrubs were
filled with birdsong and
the rustle of animals.

In autumn, the leaves
and branches crinkled and
crunched under our feet.

I used to think this forest
would always be our home.

Until the day a spark flew
across the dry treetops.

At first we didn’t notice.

The smell of smoke blew north as the flames began to grow, then turned south, toward us.

Wind made the fire roar.

Fire made the wind roar.

Our sky turned dark.

I always thought Mountain Lion was
the fiercest animal in the forest.

But like me . . .

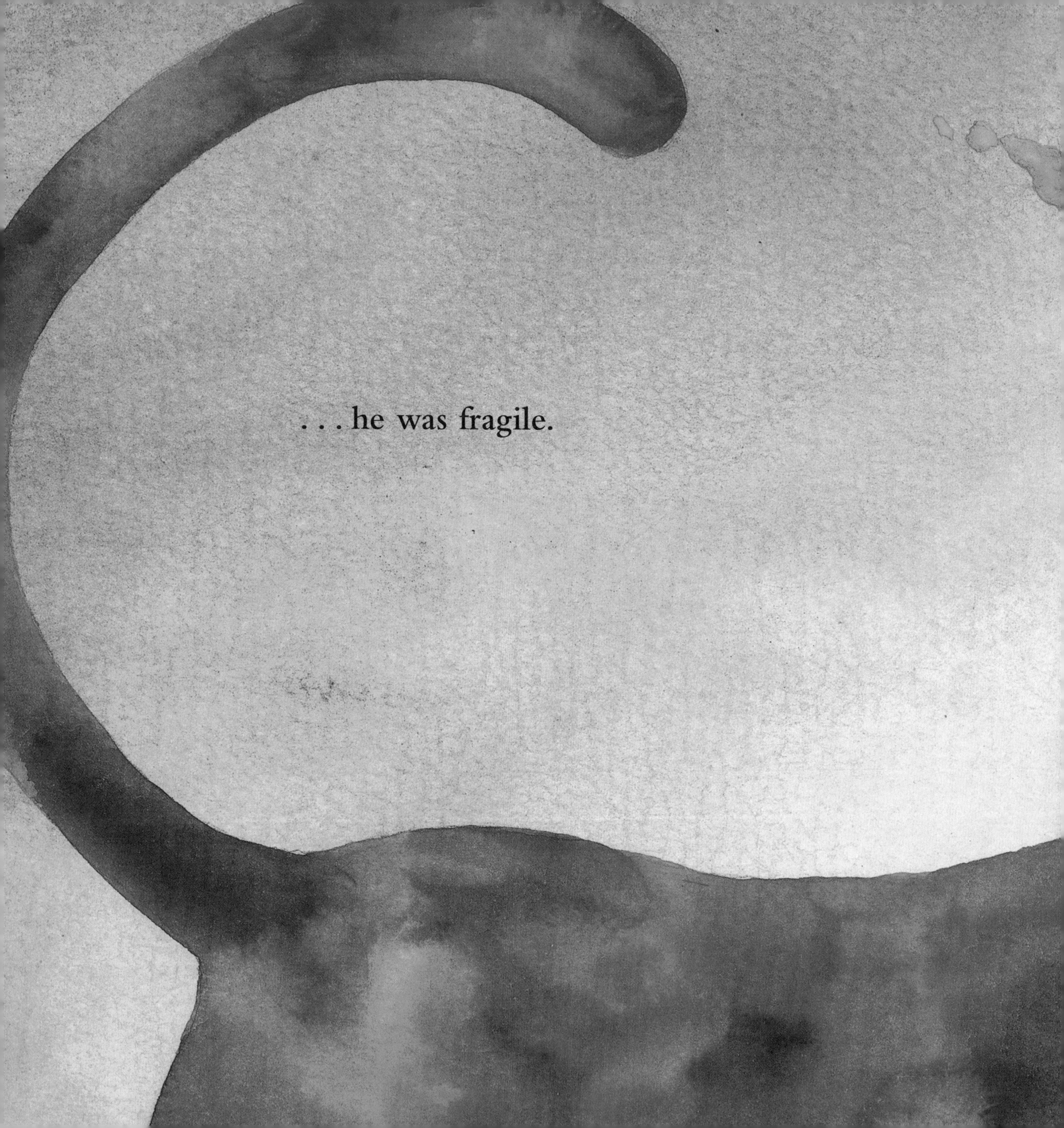

. . . he was fragile.

Before the flames swirled at us again . . .

. . . we fled.

Hot cinders spun
back and forth,

across the hills

and through the canyons.

Wind

hissed and

roared.

Fire snapped at our fur and
feathers and hooves and paws,
swallowing our trees
and blackening our sky.

When we finally stopped,
there was silence . . .

except for the cracks and
pops of fallen trees.

The smoke was strong.

But we were stronger.

In time, our forest will return.

The trees and shrubs will once
again be filled with birdsong
and the rustle of animals.

The new leaves and shoots
will be soft and quiet
under our feet.

We will live
in this forest again.

The 2017 Fires in Northern California

We Will Live in This Forest Again was inspired by the love and compassion I witnessed between complete strangers when multiple wildfires ignited across Northern California, including my hometown of Sonoma, in October 2017. The dry timber and gale-force winds quickly turned already powerful flames into a firestorm, scorching forests, grasslands, and entire neighborhoods. The wildlife, which returned soon after the fires passed through, demonstrated the strength and resilience we all needed to rebuild our lives.

Driving home late the first night of the fires, howling winds threw branches and debris across the road. Fire engines overtook me, disappearing into the smoke. Ash floated down, like falling snow. I heard propane tanks exploding to the north, louder and louder as the fire headed south, toward us. Emergency vehicles rolled through our neighborhood, loudspeakers bellowing, "EVACUATE NOW!" My flashlight darted across the walls as I gathered photos and documents. Neighbors were expressionless behind masks and bandanas wrapped across their mouths as we waved goodbye and left.

Cell-phone emergency alerts beeped and buzzed day and night, signaling continued evacuations and road closures. For days we waited while vast burning areas merged and the immense beast surrounded our little town. Time stood still in the most urgent way.

On the sixth day, our road opened to residents and we headed home. Embers the size of dinner plates littered the ashy road. We saw blackened oak trees, blackened fields, and home after home burned to nothing. Our house was spared. But many others were not. Handwritten signs posted on telephone poles read, "The love in the air is thicker than the smoke." Local residents and strangers from afar helped in any way they could, donating food and funds or tending animals that were lost or burned. When I brought a stack of picture books to the shelter, I was struck by cots lined up like little cabins, piled high with people's lives in small boxes.

As the smoke began to clear, we learned more about those painful weeks. Two hundred fifty wildfires started burning. Twenty-one became major fires that burned 245,000 acres. Eight thousand nine hundred buildings were destroyed. Forty-four people lost their lives.

Many of the research field cameras set to observe wildlife melted in the fires. But some survived and helped weave the story of how quickly the animals came home. Just two days after one area was burned, a tired buck wandered past the cameras. Two days after that, a jackrabbit and, soon after, another deer. Then a coyote, a squirrel, a mountain lion and a black bear. With the first rains in late October, once-burnt fields erupted in fresh green growth.

One year later, my brother lost his home and town in the Paradise Fire. He stayed with me as he faced this loss and took time to figure out his next steps. It was challenging, but like the animals in the forest, together, we found our way.

As I was completing the final details for this book, catastrophic wildfires were ripping through the Australian bush, highlighting the global nature of this crisis. In writing *We Will Live in This Forest Again*, I hope to show that even in the face of so much loss, over time, life will return.

Gianna Marino

Wildfire Facts

Naturally occurring wildfires play an important role in nature by burning decaying matter, keeping in check the amount of fuel on the forest floor, and returning nutrients to the soil. Prolonged drought increases the amount of fuel, causing bigger and more catastrophic fires. In the summer and fall, hot, dry winds can quickly turn these small fires into a firestorm. A firestorm is an intense and destructive fire where strong currents of air are drawn into the blaze, making it burn more fiercely.

How do wildfires start?

While some wildfires are caused by nature, most are caused by humans. Lightning, campfires, cigarettes, downed power lines, sparks from equipment, spontaneous combustion, and even train wheels striking the track on a hot, dry day can all cause a wildfire to begin. Dead trees, grasses, and forest debris are the fuel for these fires.

How do wildfires spread?

Once a fire starts, strong winds with low humidity can spread a fire quickly. These winds send embers skyward, spreading the fire faster. Temperatures can reach over 1500 degrees Fahrenheit. Wildfires need three things to burn: fuel, oxygen, and a heat source. Firefighters call these "the fire triangle." To fight wildfires, you must take away one or more of the triangle components. Wildfires can travel up to 14 miles per hour. A firestorm travels more quickly. One fire in Northern California spread at a rate of approximately 80 football fields per minute, almost 30 miles per hour.

What does wildlife do when the fire comes?

Small creatures burrow into the cooler ground or take cover under rocks. Large animals, like deer, mountain lions, or bears, will run or take refuge in streams and lakes. But not all the animals survive. Those who take shelter in a tree might be trapped. Others, who cannot move quickly enough, may not survive.

When the fire is over, animals return to find new plant growth and new feeding opportunities. With the first rains, the landscape begins to recover.

FURTHER READING

Furgang, Kathy. *Wildfires.* Washington D.C.: National Geographic Children's Books, 2015.

Simon, Seymour. *Wildfires: All About Fires, Prevention, Renewal, and More!* New York: Harper, 2016.

Thiessen, Mark, and Phelan, Glen. *Extreme Wildfire: Smoke Jumpers, High-Tech Gear, Survival Tactics, and the Extraordinary Science of Fire.* Washington D.C.: National Geographic Children's Books, 2016.

FOR MORE INFORMATION ON WILDFIRES

www.ducksters.com/science/earth_science/forest_fires.php
www.dosomething.org/facts/11-facts-about-wildfires
www.smokeybear.com/en/smokey-for-kids
www.earthtouchnews.com/natural-world/how-it-works/wildfire-and-wild-things

The author and her horse, Nobu, viewing the remains of his barn.

Were it not for first responders, neighbors, friends, strangers, and firefighters from around the world, there would be more lives lost and more homes destroyed. This book is dedicated to everyone who helped during and after the 2017 fires in Northern California.

Neal Porter Books

Printed and bound in May 2020 at Toppan Leefung, DongGuan City, China.
The artwork for this book was created using gouache on Fabriano watercolor paper.
Book design by Jennifer Browne
www.holidayhouse.com
First Edition
1 3 5 7 9 10 8 6 4 2

Library of Congress Cataloging-in-Publication Data

Names: Marino, Gianna, author, illustrator.
Title: We will live in this forest again / Gianna Marino.
Description: New York : Holiday House, [2020] | "Neal Porter Books." | Audience: Ages 3–7 | Audience: Grades K–1 | Summary: When a thriving forest is swallowed by wildfire, its residents brace themselves and look to new beginnings.
Identifiers: LCCN 2019038035 | ISBN 9780823446995 (hardcover)
Subjects: CYAC: Forest animals—Fiction. | Forest fires—Fiction.
Classification: LCC PZ7.M33882 We 2020 | DDC [E]—dc23
LC record available at https://lccn.loc.gov/2019038035